characters created by

lauren child

I'm really ever so NOT well

PUFFIN

Charlie
and
Lola™

Text based on the script written by Dave Ingham

Illustrations from the TV animation produced by Tiger Aspect

PUFFIN BOOKS
Published by the Penguin Group: London, New York, Australia,
Canada, India, Ireland, New Zealand and South Africa
Penguin Books Ltd, Registered Offices: 80 Strand, London WC2R 0RL, England

puffinbooks.com

First published 2007
Published in this edition 2008
1 3 5 7 9 10 8 6 4 2
Text and illustrations copyright © Lauren Child/Tiger Aspect Productions Limited, 2007
The Charlie and Lola logo is a trademark of Lauren Child
All rights reserved
The moral right of the author/illustrator has been asserted
Made and printed in China
ISBN: 978-1-856-13190-2

This edition produced for The Book People Ltd,
Hall Wood Avenue, Haydock, St Helens WA11 9UL

I have this little sister Lola.
She is small and very funny.
Well, usually she's very funny,
    but not when she's not feeling very well.
And today Lola's really not feeling well.

Lola has a cold.

I say, "How are you feeling, Lola?"

Lola says,
"I'm really, really
ever so **not well**,
Charlie."

So I say,
"Mum's given me some pink
milk and biscuits for you, Lola."

Pink milk is Lola's favourite.

But Lola says,

"Yuck!

My pink milk

tastes green.

And the biscuits

are too prickly

to swallow.

I don't feel like

eating or drinking

anything."

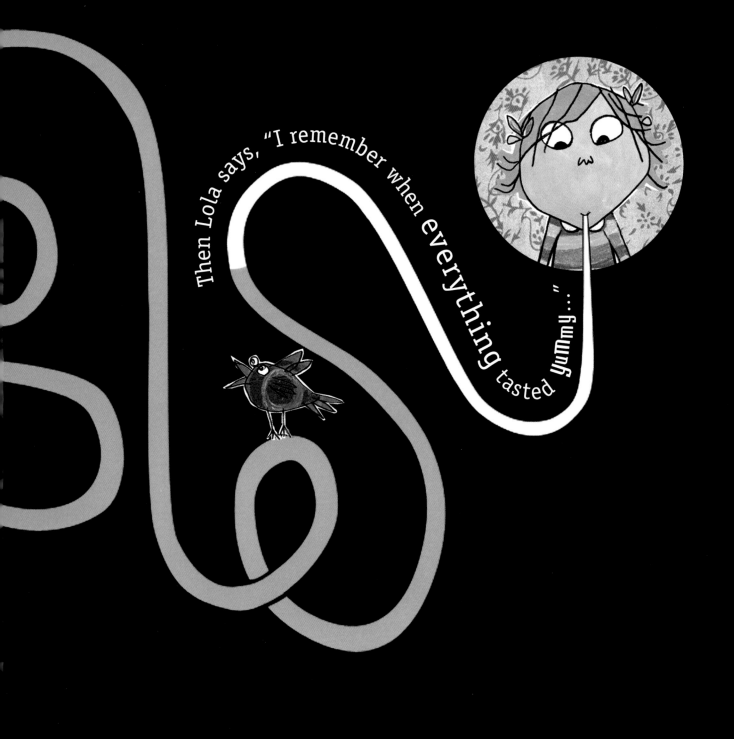

Then Lola says, "I remember when everything tasted yummy…"

So I say,
"Dad always says **flowers** are very good
at cheering little people up."

But Lola says,

"Aaaachoooooooooo!

They're not very good at
    cheering up this little person!"

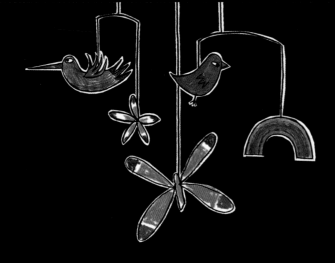

Then Lola says,

"My nose hurts,
    and nothing smells.

I remember when I used to be able to do smelling....

Then I have an idea how to cheer up Lola.

I say, "I know...
let's sing a **song**."

But Lola says,
"I can't do **singing**, Charlie...
my t**hroat** hurts and
my voice is all quiet."

Then she says, "I remember singing...

'The sun has got his hat on,

Hip, hip, hip hooray,

The sun has got his hat on

and he's coming out today!'"

Lola says,
    "Can **you** sing for me, Charlie?"

I say,
"I can't. I've got a big football game
    and I've promised Marv I'll play.
I can't break my promise."

"Pleeease, Charlie,"
    says Lola.

So I say,
"All right then...

'If you're happy

and you know it

clap

your

hands...

If you're happy and you know it clap your hands...

If you're happy and you know it,

and you really

want to show it,

If you're happy and you know it

clap your

hands!'"

Then I say,
    "You're not clapping, Lola."

"I'm not happy, Charlie," says Lola.
"Why do I feel so really, really not well?"

So I say, "It's those germs in your mouth."

"Germs?"
says Lola.

And I say,
"Your cold germs. Would you
    like to see them, Lola?"

So I take Lola
to the bathroom
    to look in the mirror.

Lola says,

"Ahhhhhhhhhhhh..."

Then I hear the phone ringing.
I say,
"It's probably Marv.
I'd better go and answer it."

Marv says,
"So, are you coming
to play football then?
It's a big game, you know!"

I say,
"Yes, it's just that Lola..."

"Charlieee!
I feel really, really
terribly **eVer so**
NOT well,"

says Lola.

And I say,
"I've just told Marv that
        I'm on my way. Mum says
    she'll come and play with you."

And Lola says,
    "But I want you
to play with me, Charlie!"

    So I say, "Okay.
    How about a quick jigsaw puzzle?"

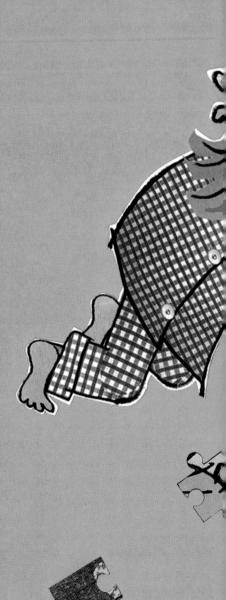

The smiley puzzle
is Lola's favourite.

Then I hear the phone
ringing again
and I know
it's going
to be Marv...

Marv says,
"So you're definitely
coming then?"

I say,
"Of course I am...
I'm coming...
right now!"

Lola says,
"Charlie! I want you
to stay...

Please?"

And then I have a really good idea.
"Hey, Lola," I say.
"Where's your butterfly gone...?"

"To Flutterby Mountain!" says Lola.

"Yes," I say.
"Do you want to try and catch him?"

Lola says,
"Do you think we can
catch Mr Butterfly?"

"Quickly," I say,

"we're going to have to... cloud hop!"

Lola says, "I love cloud hopping, Charlie."

"Come here, fluttery butterfly,"
says Lola.
"Let me catch you..."

Then I hear
a knock at the door.

"Come on, Charlie!"
says Marv.

And I say,
"All ri...

Ah...

Ah...

Ah...

The next day, I'm in bed feeling really not well.
Lola says, "So, how are you feeling, Charlie?"

I say,
"I'm really... really
not well, Lola!"

And Lola says,
"Don't worry,
Charlie...

...because I'm going to be here every
minute of all day until you're
completely absolutely **better!**"

And I say,
    "Every minute of all day...
    Muuummm!"